This Little Tiger book belongs to:

_____

_____

_____

For Gussie, forever in our hearts . . . ~T.C.

For Piddle Valley Preschool ~ J.C.

LITTLE TIGER PRESS LTD.
an imprint of the Little Tiger Group
1 Coda Studios 189 Munster Road, London SW6 6AW
Imported into the EEA by Penguin Random House Ireland,
Morrison Chambers, 32 Nassau Street, Dublin D02 YH68
www.littletiger.co.uk
First published in Great Britain 2010
This edition published 2020
Text copyright © Tracey Corderoy 2010, 2020
Illustrations copyright © Jane Chapman 2010
Visit Jane Chapman at www.janekchapman.com
Tracey Corderoy and Jane Chapman have asserted their rights
to be identified as the author and illustrator of this work
under the Copyright, Designs and Patents Act, 1988
A CIP catalogue record for this book is available
from the British Library • All rights reserved

ISBN 978-1-78881-801-8 • LTP/2700/3981/0521
Manufactured, printed, and assembled in Foshan, China.
Fourth printing, May 2021
4 6 8 10 9 7 5

The Little White Owl

by Tracey Corderoy   Illustrated by Jane Chapman

LITTLE TIGER

LONDON

Once there was a little white owl who
lived by himself in the snow. He didn't
have a mother. He didn't have a father.
He didn't **even** have a name.

But he didn't really mind too much.
It had **always** been like that.
And his head was **full**
of happy stories.

Sometimes he was a brave white knight . . .

and sometimes he was a snowflake.

Sometimes he was a rocket, blasting off to the moon!

But every night, at bedtime, he sat on a **high** branch, nibbling toast and counting the stars, by himself.

Then one day, he looked at the big, blue sky that stretched on and on forever . . .

"I wonder what's out there?" said the little white owl.

So he packed his teddy and his clock. It was time to see the world!

For days the little white owl flew—
over turquoise oceans and deserts of gold.
Then he spotted the **prettiest** trees,
sprinkled with tiny jewels, so down, down,
down he swooped—**but wait** . . .

. . . these jewels had beaks! They were owls—
beautiful owls! Owls just like him!
"Would anyone like a bite of toast?" he said.

But the beautiful owls sat quiet and still.
They didn't want to spoil their perfect feathers.
"How very plain you are," groaned the green.
"No patterns at all," sniffed the dotty red.
"You don't belong with us. GO AWAY!"

"But I do have a sparkle!" cried the little white owl.
"Here—in my heart! And bumping up and
down in me are lots of happy stories. I'll share
them with you if you want me to!"

The owls sat and thought, then.
"Hmmm . . ." sighed the blue.

"A story might help pass the time."

"Fine, but just **one**," said

the flowery pink with a yawn.

So the little white owl swung on
a branch with his little teddy.
And he munched his toast and
shared a happy story.

"Aaahhhhh . . ." breathed
the blue owl dreamily when the
little white owl had finished.
The other owls all glared at her.
"Ooops, sorry!" she blushed.
"But couldn't we have just one more?"

So the little white owl closed his eyes and magical stories came pouring from his heart. Wonderful tales of castles and knights and dragons with fiery breath . . .

and blasting through
moonbeams and counting
bright stars and tumbling
down like a snowflake!

Slowly, and rather to their surprise, the owls began to smile. "Aaahhhhh . . ." they breathed. Then suddenly, "MORE!" everyone cried.

At last, when all his toast was gone, the little white owl checked his clock. "Gosh, I need to go!" he gasped. "Back to my sparkly home. I need to feel the snow and count the stars . . ."
But then . . .

... a blue wing fluttered and a tail of dotty red began to twitch ...

"Take us too!" cried the pretty owls, sweeping into the sky. "We want to feel your fluffy snow and count your sparkly stars. And play . . . and laugh . . . and tumble—just like you!"

So the little white owl led them home
where they tumbled and twirled on the ice.
Like splashes of rainbow they speckled
the snow, their patterns brighter than ever!

Later, they huddled together and sipped warm cocoa.
"Tomorrow, when we fly home," said the blue,
"the white clouds will remind us of you! Promise
you'll visit very soon!"

"I promise," smiled the little white owl,
"and you can tell me all **your** stories."
Then he snuggled up on his branch . . .

...and soon was dreaming happy
dreams, as a huge, silver moon lit
the deep, dark sky that stretched
on and on **forever** ...